HARKHUF

The First Explorer

By Laura Marshall

Cover illustration © Alexander Singleton

Soft cover ISBN 978-0-9957131-1-6

Cover illustration by Alexander Singleton at Hunting Town Design

Back cover design by Lucy Norman at STUDIO MAKECREATE

Edited by Sophie Playle at Liminal Pages

Photography by James Marshall

This novel is a work of fiction and the characters and events in it exist only in its pages and in the author's imagination.

"Welcome in peace, have a good journey."
Pyramid Texts

Contents

Prologue

1. Harkhuf: Island Boy
2. Zau: City Slicker
3. Harkhuf: A Visit from Merenra
4. Zau: Waiting for the Boy
5. Harkhuf: Meeting the Nubians
6. Zau: Injustice
7. Harkhuf: Festival of Wag
8. Harkhuf: The Journey Begins
9. Zau: Island Life
10. Harkhuf: Striking Gold
11. Harkhuf: The Red Land
12. Zau: Hide and Seker
13. Harkhuf: Kingdom of Kerma
14. Zau: Charity
15. Harkhuf: Bes
16. Zau: Sickening for Something
17. Harkhuf: Where the Two Rivers Meet
18. Harkhuf: Return from Kerma
19. Harkhuf: A Hundred Friends

Epilogue

Character list

Harkhuf	Fourteen year old-boy
Iry	Harkhuf's father
Wadi	Harkhuf's best friend
Nepthys	Wadi's sister
Nizam	Harkhuf's childhood friend
Seker	Harkhuf's falcon
Pharaoh Merenra	6th Dynasty Pharaoh
Queen Ankhesen	Pharaoh's wife
Seneni	Pharaoh's priest
Uni	Pharaoh's chief governor
Zau	Uni's son
Gamal	Zau's friend
Nemeh	A Nubian chief
Midou and Hasan	Soldiers
Greywacke	Harkhuf's donkey
Thutma	Baker's wife
Bes	Tiny scorpion charmer
Pepi II	The baby prince
Tepi	Famous harpist

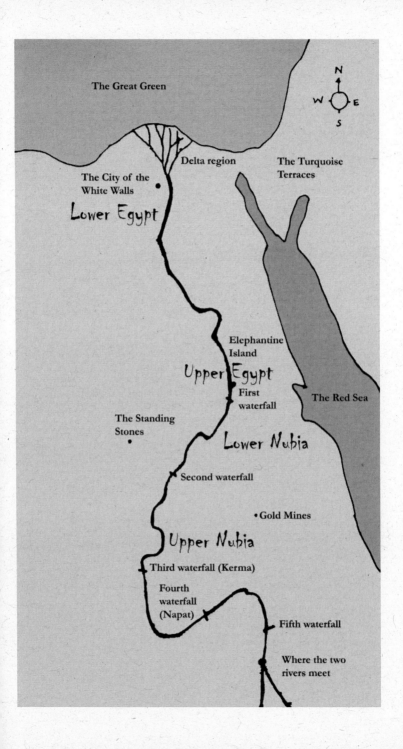

Prologue

This is not the story of Tutankhamun or Cleopatra. It is not the tale of Rameses and Nefertiti. Harkhuf's story begins long before these pharaohs and queens ruled, when Egypt was known as the Black Land and the River Nile was known as the Iteru. There were no camels, no cars and no tourists travelling along the riverside. There weren't very many pyramids either.

One year during Akhet – the flooding season – the banks of the river were almost dry. On Elephantine Island in the far south, Harkhuf and his father, Iry, watched the falling water level in horror. Was Khnum, the river god, sending a drought as punishment? All around, green was turning to brown and earth was turning to dust. The threat of starvation loomed across the Black Land like a shadow. Panic began to set in.

Further north, in the City of the White Walls, Pharaoh Merenra desperately asked his priest, Seneni, what to do.

"Send gifts to the gods!" Seneni cried.

The pharaoh wasted no time in making his plans. He ordered his chief governor, Uni, to build a royal barge.

"The floods will come, the floods will come," the pharaoh said to all who asked. He didn't want the people of the Black Land to know that he feared for their lives.

1

Harkhuf: Island Boy

My grandmother chose my name for me. I'm the only boy named Harkhuf on the island. It means "protected by Horus". I like the idea of being watched over by the god of skies and kings. There are definitely worse things to be named after.

At festival time, my grandmother would always say, "A small house can lodge a hundred friends." And her favourite saying of all: "A beautiful thing is never perfect." It's not true of course.

My best friend, Wadi, is beautiful and perfect. She isn't proud like the other island girls. She's real. Wadi always said I should be an explorer.

Not all my friends are so supportive. Nizam thinks it's funny that my best friend is a girl. He would be my best friend himself if he wasn't so immature. Nizam's dad is the baker. Before Nizam and I fell out, we would spend hours at the bakery, just watching his dad mould the dough. Nizam's dad is less serious than my dad. It's a shame his friendly nature hasn't rubbed off on his son. Nizam was the first person to make me feel bad about my facial hair. I've always had a lot more face fluff than anyone else my age, and it's thick too – on my face and chest. I began shaving early, but little patches of hair spring up again after just a few hours.

Anyway, enough about Nizam. He's not that important.

I remember the day when Dad and I stood at the base of the steps leading up from the river and he first alerted me to the coming drought. We were expecting the first visit from Pharaoh Merenra and his wife, Queen Ankhesen, on the royal barge. No one could quite believe that the pharaoh wanted to leave his palace to visit our tiny island in Ta-Sety, the Land of the Bow.

Our island is one of a kind. We call it Elephantine Island because its bulky cliffs look like elephants. Life here is simple most of the time. I've always been popular with the other boys but when I was younger I would often spend time alone, daydreaming about what might lie beyond our banks. I longed for adventure, something out of the ordinary. I didn't want to become like my dad. Not that I dislike my dad, not at all. My dad taught me pretty much everything I know. He showed me how to catch fish and how to lead a caravan of donkeys, which is harder than it sounds. You have to be gentle and it takes patience. Nizam definitely couldn't do it.

Not all of what Dad taught me was fun or even interesting. I suffered his less exciting lessons politely, telling myself that one day they might be useful. Besides, I didn't want to hurt his feelings. He showed me how to record the water level, which was one of his most important jobs as governor. The water level affects how much tax is collected for the pharaoh, so Dad always prayed for a perfect flood, not too little and not so much as to drown all the crops.

The island isn't very large. There are enough houses for the hundred or so people that live here and most of those are clumped together in the centre. There are two temples, one for Khnum, the river god, and one for his wife, Satet. That's pretty much it, apart from the bakery. But Elephantine Island would always be my home. Yes, I wanted adventure, but I also wanted something to come back to. Looking back, I sometimes wonder if the adventure was worth all the trouble.

2

Zau: City Slicker

Living near the palace has its plus points. Yes, the City of the White Walls stinks. It stinks of donkey droppings, stagnant water and dust. But there aren't many places in the Black Land where you can get rich quick. Sell something pretty you've made to the palace and you can feed yourself for a whole month. Become a regular crafter and you can start to really make it.

I remember the first time I helped Father with a job for the pharaoh. I was about six years old and not very useful to have around. Father's job was to choose men that were strong enough to go to war. People had come from all over to go through the selection process. I was "helping" Father by collecting the arrows after the shooting test.

One afternoon, Father went to have a lie down. It had been punishingly hot and he was happy to leave me outside chasing birds. Once he was safely asleep, I grabbed one of the bows and decided to have a go for myself. The target had to be something low. I desperately wanted to fire that arrow and, drawing back the bow, I knew I didn't have long before my fingers would give way. The first thing that caught my eye was a wild cat. I was so scared that Father would wake to see me playing with the bow that I fired the arrow without thinking. It hit the cat directly in the eye.

The sight was repulsive. Blood oozed from the socket. What a pathetic creature it was, so easily hunted by a child. I took off my shirt and wrapped the cat's body in it. I had to hide the evidence before anyone saw. I dug a shallow grave and threw the cat in before filling the hole back up again.

They say cats are sacred, that they contain human souls. I had seen this one roaming around the White Walls plenty of times. It didn't seem special to me. You could see the fleas dancing on its sleek brown and copper coat. But I haven't been able to look at a cat since without remembering the trouble I caused. Father was none the wiser.

That was nearly ten years ago. I've helped out with many jobs for the pharaoh since then: painting, building, you name it. I don't like the pharaoh. I find him patronising. All the women of the Black Land make lotions from mandrake flowers and honey in an attempt to be as beautiful as the queen. But the pharaoh is as bald as a Nubian vulture and almost as ugly.

My friend Gamal works as a domestic servant in the palace. Apparently Pharaoh Merenra has been calling out in his sleep about scorpions. That's got to be bad, right? Father told me it means there is a drought coming. He said that hundreds of years ago there was a Pharaoh called Netjerikhet – or something like that – who had also dreamed of scorpions, and afterwards there was a really bad drought. Thousands of people died. Maybe the people of the Black Land have it coming.

Now Father tells me we've got to go all the way to Elephantine Island with the pharaoh. I can't imagine why. It's going to be a really long journey along the Iteru. I wonder if it's possible to die of boredom.

3

Harkhuf: A Visit from Merenra

On the morning of the pharaoh's arrival, I sat at the edge of the island with my feet dangling in the river. I had checked the water level and realised Dad was right. This was getting serious. It was already the middle of the first month of Akhet and yet the water level had not risen at all. If anything, it was slightly lower. I wasn't worried though. There had been some terrible droughts when my grandmother was a child – and she had been okay.

I could see Seker in the nearby mountains, circling for her first meal of the day. She landed by the river, took a drink and then soared off again.

I had taken her in when she was just a fledgling. Her wing was broken so I fastened a twig to it using some cloth to make a splint. It took several weeks to heal properly. I had to find food for her and I felt a bit guilty raiding a kingfisher nest, but it was worth it. Seker grew into a magnificent falcon. My father and I trained her to carry small objects tied to her leg and we sometimes used her to carry messages to nearby villages. She was a great pet, independent and yet always loyal. She never went away for very long. The island girls loved her. Wadi had even tried to paint her, but she wouldn't sit still.

Wadi loved to paint and sculpt. She was so excited about the royal visit. She had lined the temple with sacred offerings: jugs filled with wine and decorated with hieroglyphs of Osiris. It was coming up to the Festival of Wag, and soon the Iteru would be filled with rafts carrying statues and food fit for the pharaoh.

I was strangely nervous, but the rhythm of the river calmed me. Once I was ready, I rose to my feet and began to clamber awkwardly up the narrow steps to the temple of Khnum, where I found my dad hunched over in prayer.

"Morning, Dad," I called.

"Good morning, son," he replied, without looking up.

"Not in a festival mood?"

"Festival? Oh, the Festival of Wag, you mean."

How could Dad have forgotten the festival? Wadi's shrill voice interrupted my thoughts.

"Merenra Nemtyemsaf is here! And his beautiful queen!"

I helped Dad up and we stepped out of the temple into the heat of the day. A dizzy feeling hit me. I couldn't see the boats because of the angle of the rock face, but the three of us began to make our way through the shaded grove and down the stone steps towards the jetty. The villagers were already there to greet the pharaoh and his party, with offerings of fresh bread and pomegranate wine. A local girl adorned Queen Ankhesen with a lotus flower garland. As we got closer, I could see that the queen was heavy with child.

Dad picked up the pace as we neared the jetty, where he and I knelt before the pharaoh. The crowd hushed. They wanted to hear everything.

"Loyal and humble governor, Iry," the pharaoh said, addressing Dad, "servant to the people of Elephantine Island – please rise."

We stood. The pharaoh continued in a cracked, quiet voice. "May we speak privately? This is a matter of some urgency."

Dad looked over his shoulder at the crowds. He licked his lips as if his mouth was dry.

"Most reverend Pharaoh Merenra Antyemsaf, descended from Osiris the Great himself. This is my son, Harkhuf. Although his ears are still young, they are the ears of tomorrow. I urge you to allow him to be present at our meeting."

The pharaoh frowned. I lowered my eyes. *Don't look at me.*

"As I have no son of my own, forgive me if I do not understand this bond of yours," the pharaoh said.

"Then may I suggest that we retire to the temple of Satet, where we will not be bothered by well-wishers?" asked Dad.

The pharaoh paused, and then said, "Not before I have introduced you to somebody."

My eyes wandered to two unfamiliar faces in the crowd: an ageing man and a boy who was probably a few years older than me.

The pharaoh ushered the newcomers forward and I couldn't help but stare.

"May I present Uni, my most dutiful minister. And this is his son, Zau," said Pharaoh Merenra.

I bowed.

"Uni has been preparing the waterways for bigger boats. His son Zau has been helping him," continued the pharaoh. "They have come to show me the river."

"They are our welcome guests," said Dad as he gestured uphill towards the temple and led the pharaoh away.

The temple of Satet was not as impressive as the temple of Khnum, and I knew Wadi was upset that the pharaoh would not see her offerings. She hadn't said a word since we left the temple. Even so, she was amazed to have the opportunity to speak with Queen Ankhesen, who had stayed at the jetty. The queen addressed the crowds, who were burning with questions. *Why have you graced our island? How do you get your hair so shiny?* I felt my face go red. Why did they have to be so nosey?

"We have come to Elephantine Island to meet with Nubian rulers and be blessed by them. And yet, there is another more pressing reason for our long journey," the queen said.

I was guessing it had nothing to do with her hair. I stood next to Wadi and heard her voice rise above the others.

"What is the reason, divine Queen?"

Excitement hung in the air.

"Unfortunately, I cannot tell you."

A low moan came from the crowd, but Queen Ankhesen's tone stopped any further questions. I watched as Dad and the pharaoh continued to climb towards the opening of the temple. Dad was stooped over, weighed down by his thoughts. The new boy, Zau, stood next to me, whispering with his dad. They were looking at large scrolls of papyrus. As I approached, they rolled up the scrolls and made their way onto the royal barge. Perhaps the royal visit was more serious than I had thought.

4

Zau: Waiting for the Boy

Father dragged me along to Elephantine Island with the pharaoh as arranged. The barge trip was tedious. Seneni, the pharaoh's priest, was at the queen's side to protect her from evil spirits. The river is full of them, after all.

We passed endless cubits of similar scenery, nothing I hadn't seen before. Reeds, lotuses, reeds, lotuses. Even the crocodiles were uninspiring as they lurked at the water's edge. I was tempted to join the oarsmen and their rowing, just to have something to do. I watched as their strong limbs pushed and dragged, pushed and dragged, their brown bodies glistening with the tiniest beads of sweat.

As we neared the island, Pharaoh Merenra became fidgety. He paced the deck. Just a few nights on the barge had turned him into a grey-faced ruin. I was restless too. I wasn't allowed to know anything about the reasons for the trip. I was just a kid after all. I had given up trying to persuade Father or the pharaoh to see me as anything other than that. I was there to observe, to learn, to be seen and not heard. The fact that I wasn't strong enough to be a soldier meant that I was only good for one thing, and that was following in the footsteps of Father. Unless I could find another way to make a living, that is.

When we arrived on the island, the pharaoh left us to entertain ourselves whilst he spoke with Iry, the governor of the region. Queen Ankhesen did her best to keep everyone quiet but they were a noisy lot. I had the pleasure of her company for over an hour once the locals had begun to make their way back to their homes. When the pharaoh returned from his long chat with Iry, I was put on babysitting duty – I was to chaperone the governor's son, Harkhuf. Well, I couldn't say no, even though I hate hanging around with younger kids. They cling to you like leeches. They always think their friends will be impressed that they know someone older and more experienced. The last thing I wanted to do was spend time with scrawny little Harkhuf. Just because both our fathers are governors, everyone thinks we should get on really well.

The pharaoh sent me to wait for the boy on the jetty. Seriously, how long does it take for one boy to get washed and dressed? There's nothing worse than vanity. How long must he spend styling his hair?

Having a sidelock is so much better. Hair never gets in your face.

The island people seem kind of simple. Life is very different in the City of the White Walls. More hustle and bustle. I can't imagine anything interesting ever happening on Elephantine Island. Visiting the place is like going back in time. The mud brick houses are so basic. It would be better to live in the palace prison than those little huts.

As I waited, a wasp flew circles around me. It would not give up. I batted it away. The royal party was about to set off to meet with the Nubians. They would leave without both of us if Harkhuf didn't hurry up! I decided to catch up on some reading whilst I waited. I unrolled one of the maps that Father had given me. The only interesting parts were marked with black crosses, where the gold mines were supposed to be. The rest was just a blur.

5

Harkhuf: Meeting the Nubians

Wadi came to see me after Dad returned from the temple. Queen Ankhesen had asked her to create a birth brick for the coming prince or princess. She was keen to get started straight away, practising prayers and spells. I noticed she was wearing a new cotton *kalasiri*, and she hadn't brushed her hair, which fell down in cascades. She wanted to hear everything. Had I spoken to my dad? What did the pharaoh want? Was there some danger? I shrugged off her questions, pretending I knew nothing. The queen had stirred up an enormous amount of gossip and I wasn't about to stoke that fire.

Of course, Dad had told me that the pharaoh was sending him to Nubia. That's not the sort of thing he would keep from me, even if he had sworn an oath of secrecy. Nothing beats the family bond, at least not for the two of us. But why? Why would the pharaoh want Dad to travel so many thousands of cubits? I couldn't get the answer out of him but he did tell me he would meet with the Nubian chiefs at the border that evening to discuss plans.

"And there's more," he murmured.

I took in a breath.

"I *will* be relying on you to carry out duties in my absence."

"For how long?" I asked. My voice quivered.

He moved closer and ruffled my hair. "Fear is our greatest enemy," he said. "You know that. Meet me at the jetty at sundown."

Before I could argue with him, he had gone. Dad could be cryptic sometimes. We got on better if I didn't ask too many questions. He liked to leave things unanswered, usually so he could claim to be right. I had no idea why he wanted me to meet him at the jetty. I put it down to one of his whims.

As soon as Wadi had gone, I washed, prayed and checked the water level for a second time that day. Stepping out of my chamber, my mood shifted. The sun's rays began to soften and disappear behind the dunes. I kicked the ground as I walked. Why wasn't I trusted to travel to Nubia? How could I run an island when I had so little experience? I had never even left Ta-Sety, let alone the Black Land.

Dad was not at the jetty. Uni's son, Zau, greeted me instead. He was taller than me and skinnier. His nose was slim and crooked and his eyes

27

were too narrow. He wore a short *shendyt* like me but his hair was in a sidelock. It was strange seeing a sidelock on a boy so close to my age. Only little children wear their hair like that on the island.

Zau seemed impatient.

"The elders are on the boat," he said.

The elders? What language was he speaking?

"Your father is on the boat with the pharaoh," Zau persisted. "Come, you may visit him now that his important meeting is over."

Zau gestured to the barge and I stepped on awkwardly, nearly falling into the gap between the jetty and the side of the boat. The barge was thicker and stronger than the rafts my dad and I used to get around the islands, but I almost lost my balance. Zau sniggered.

My forced smile became a grimace and I stumbled towards the centre of the barge. My vision was blurred by a mosquito net, but I could see Dad under the wooden shelter talking to Queen Ankhesen. The boat was quite luxurious. Platters of food were laid out, with fruit carved into the shapes of birds. One of the servants had even folded the napkins to look like crocodiles. I made my way over, admiring the craftsmanship.

Dad was unusually jolly and there were dark stains on the sides of his lips. Wine always made his cheeks go scarlet, and I flashed him a smile.

"You're coming with us to meet the Nubian chiefs," he said, slightly louder than necessary.

Wadi was never going to believe me! The barge got moving and I marvelled again at the variety of birds dipping, darting, hovering and lurking over the water. I had not seen Seker since that morning, but I knew she would keep an eye on us and protect us from harm. A couple of hours later, we reached the waterfall dividing the Black Land and Nubia and saw a group of Nubians waiting. A strange creature, something like a horse, but with a long neck and large patches of white and brown fur, was grazing next to them. It was from another world. On the dunes, men banged drums while others danced and shouted. I stood next to the pharaoh. He smiled, the wrinkles around his black eyes like small deltas.

Zau led the way off the barge. It was a short climb to where the Nubians were gathered. My father greeted the men warmly. He had picked up some Nubian words whilst dealing with the people of Ta-Sety. They had no trouble understanding him. One of the chiefs, Nemeh, began to lead a ritual dance.

His energy was awesome! He beckoned the pharaoh to join him, but Merenra resisted and ushered me and Zau forward instead.

Zau was sheepish. He didn't have much in the way of coordination, but Nemeh wouldn't take no for an answer. He paced up and down on the spot as he spoke. Each time he chanted a word, we were expected to repeat it. The rest of the royal party stood and watched. They couldn't help being amused at my attempts to perform the chant. Thankfully Nemeh realised that they were sniggering at me and not at him. I don't have a natural sense of rhythm.

After what seemed like a lifetime of marching and shouting, the Nubian chiefs bowed first to the pharaoh and then to me. We feasted together by an open fire, passing plates of food around like old friends. My father and Uni translated for the pharaoh as best as they could. The strange horse I had seen was a gift for him. He was then presented with beautiful leopard hides and some incense sticks, which they showed us how to burn safely. By this time, the sun was well and truly out of sight. The pharaoh promised that he would soon be sending gifts from the Black Land and explained that my father would be making a journey into Nubia.

Nemeh was pleased, but he also had a warning for the pharaoh. Rebel warriors had been setting up camps along the water's edge and were not to be trusted.

I glanced at my father and saw the creases in his forehead deepen. "Both Harkhuf and I are happy to assist you in any way you feel is right," he said to Pharaoh Merenra.

"Your Majesty, I echo Iry's words," said Uni.

Pharaoh Merenra looked grateful. But a cloud of worry hung over him. "Then Harkhuf will go with Iry to Nubia," he said at last.

"Perhaps Zau would be a better choice," suggested Uni.

I drew in a breath.

The pharaoh was not offended, but quickly responded.

"Zau shall take over the running of Elephantine Island."

My mouth made a sound that was something like a baby cooing. I coughed to disguise it, but I couldn't conceal the redness of my face. Zau's eyelids twitched and his eyes narrowed into ill-lit caverns. I couldn't believe the pharaoh trusted him to run our island. If it wasn't for my thirst for adventure, I probably would have said something then.

Pharaoh Merenra and his party dropped me and Dad back at the island on their journey back to the City of the White Walls. It didn't feel real. The pharaoh wanted me to go to Nubia! Dad didn't want to stay up and talk like we normally did. I watched the stars and thanked the gods for my good fortune. I was going to be an explorer at last.

6

Zau: Injustice

I knew Harkhuf would turn out to be a thorn in my side. Snorting like that when he heard it would be me running their precious island. Who does he think he is? Even the queen was in favour of him going on the trip to Nubia. Injustice makes even the most beautiful of things appear ugly.

After the lanky boy had finally been dropped back at the island, I remained with the boat party whilst we journeyed north, back to the capital. There were a couple of stop-offs planned along the way.

Indeed, the pharaoh was full of plans. He was convinced he needed to finish building his tomb as soon as possible. I was expected to help Father organise the movement of alabaster stone from the south back up to the City of the White Walls. Is there anything a pharaoh won't do to flatter the gods? When I realised quite how much work there was to do, I was determined to get out of it. Lugging stone slabs around after an already long and tedious journey is not my idea of fun. I've never been much of an actor, but I managed to convince the entire barge party that I wanted to start my role as temporary governor as soon as possible. Forced enthusiasm is the only language anyone seems to understand.

The plan was agreed. Queen Ankhesen thought I was brave for agreeing to swim back to Elephantine Island from the barge. In the dark too! We were moored on the opposite side to the island, and it was going to take me a good hour to swim the width of the river and then several more do the rest of the journey on foot. I'm not completely fearless, but I do thrive on danger. Nothing comes of playing it safe. That's how I knew the pharaoh had made the wrong choice in Harkhuf. As it turned out, I wasn't the only one who thought the pharaoh had made a big mistake. I couldn't sit back and let the fate of the Black Land fall into the hands of a child and his weak-willed father. I had to do something, even if it took me weeks to get it organised.

There's something magical about the stretch of the river just north of the island. Not far from there, on the west bank, is a dune that Father and I had climbed countless times before. I used to love running down it, with the sand scorching the soles of my feet before I dipped them in the river. I thought about making a detour but there was too much to get done.

The water was cold but that has never bothered me. I swam slowly, occasionally turning on to my back to see the stars better. My thoughts returned to my conversation with the pharaoh's priest, Seneni, on the barge:

"Can I trust you, Zau?" he asked.

I assured him he could, and he continued in the same mysterious vein.

"The pharaoh needs help. The only way to please the gods – and bring back the floods – is to make a sacrifice. But he won't do it. He's too squeamish."

"It would have to be somebody valuable in the eyes of the gods," I replied. Seneni thought Iry was the best choice and I couldn't really argue.

"Do you need some help?" I asked.

"I'll need more than that," he said. "I will need your wits and your word."

It was a small price to pay for revenge.

"Here, take these," Seneni had said, handing me some precious turquoise stones. I wasn't expecting payment, but Seneni explained that I might have a few expenses along the way.

When at last I reached the east bank, I found a soldier on duty by the river. We needed a way to make the offering quietly, and this soldier - who called himself Has - was surprisingly easy to bribe.

7

Harkhuf: Festival of Wag

Dad was in brighter spirits the next morning as he left
to buy gifts for the Nubian chiefs. I still didn't know
why on earth we were being sent so far away but I
didn't want to ask too many questions. Besides, I had
plenty to distract me. It was the first day of the
Festival of Wag – one of my favourite celebrations in
the calendar. It's a time when we remember those who
have passed into Duat, and it is the only time of year
when I feel slightly close to my mother. Villagers tell
me stories about her, what she had been like as a
young girl. Everyone says I look just like her. I never
saw her face so I don't know how true that is, but
sometimes I feel her watching over me.

Festival time is always fun, but the water level was
playing on my mind. I clambered down the steps to
see if there had been any change. Just one false foot
would have spelled disaster. People said that the
steps had been carved by the great architect Imhotep
himself, who had built the Step Pyramid at Sakkara.
I think he probably did a better job of the pyramid.

I looked down at the water. The Iteru barely reached the bottom step, and I prayed that our mission might be the solution to the problem.

Glancing round to the jetty, I saw the ritual rafts being loaded. The rafts we used were quite small, no wider than the trunk of an acacia tree. After climbing back up the steps, I weaved back down between the trees. The islanders were choosing their offerings for Osiris. Wadi had laid out her clay creations on a cotton cloth. She handed me a small statue of a falcon and then picked up a larger carving of Nut – the sky goddess – with her arms spread wide to protect the world. Together, we took the offerings down to the jetty and placed them on the rafts that would soon make their way downriver.

"You will be there for the dance at sunset, won't you?" Wadi asked me.

"What dance?" I asked teasingly.

She looked hurt.

"Of course. I wouldn't miss the biggest dance of the season!" I assured her.

I had no idea how I was I going to tell her I was leaving.

*

Dad arrived back from his shopping trip late that afternoon, bringing with him a caged viper and a bird that looked like a pink ibis. I had never seen such a bird before. It must have come all the way from the delta region. The Nubian chiefs were bound to be impressed. Dad was a priest as well as a governor, and he had an eye for detail. The pharaoh had given him some special amulets too. There was a wooden ankh – the symbol of life – and some emeralds. Dad said the pharaoh wanted us to lay them at the "true source" of the Iteru. The true source? Wasn't that on the island? Maybe the river was longer than people realised. I was beginning to guess what this journey was all about. Was the drought really that bad after all?

I didn't have time to check with Dad because as he was showing me the amulets, Zau popped his head around the door. We weren't expecting to show him around the island as we didn't think he would arrive until after we had started our trip. But since he was there, Dad decided we would need to spend the rest of the day showing him where everything was kept and introducing him to everyone he needed to know. Would I ever get to talk to Wadi?

Once Zau had been shown how to take the water reading and record it, we were free to get ourselves ready for the evening's celebrations. We left Zau to unpack his belongings and walked down to the clearing in the trees on the western side of the island, which was used for large gatherings. Oil lamps had been lit and the island women were just finishing off wreaths of olive and acacia leaves to be sent along the Iteru towards the tombs of the pharaohs further north. Low wooden tables were laden with stewed goose with prunes and fish with sweet potato.

Dad let me try some pomegranate wine. If I was old enough to go to Nubia, I was old enough to have a drink, he said. I had tasted wine before but not properly. The first sip was horrible. It was strong and sickly, but then Dad told me to taste the grape wine. He said it was drier and would taste nicer with the goose. He was right. After a few bigger gulps and a helping of goose, I was feeling happy. We were some of the first people to arrive. Wadi and her sister, Nepthys, were still rehearsing their dance in the clearing. I called out words of encouragement, not that they appreciated it very much. They seemed to be struggling to coordinate part of the dance, and I was distracting them.

Zau joined us as Nizam and his family arrived. Zau had some pomegranate wine. He liked the sweeter stuff. Nizam wasn't allowed any because he had to be up early to help with the baking. I didn't even need to brag. The look on his face when he saw me sipping from a goblet was priceless.

We all watched Wadi and Nepthys's dance. Somehow they had managed to make the trickier bits seem easy. Even Zau cheered as they flung petals at the crowds and came to join us, leaving the musicians playing. Wadi kept saying I was drunk but I didn't embarrass myself. I only had a couple of goblets. Wadi seemed to like Zau, and I was beginning to think he wasn't that bad after all. Nepthys teased him for his sidelock and he took it in good humour. Both girls wanted to hear about life in the capital city. I knew both of them would be happy to leave the island to start a new life there. From what Zau said, it sounded dirty and noisy.

Dad and I stayed up later than we should have. Perhaps

to remember Elephantine Island at its best. I lost track of time. It was like being a kid again. Nizam didn't even get on my nerves. We played *senet* and I won as I always did. Zau had never played it before. I guess they have different games in the city.

We stayed up until the sky was shrouded with grey and blue. The hooting of owls could be heard, and the cheerful daytime birdsong had died away. Wadi and I were the last to make our way home. It was chilly and I gave her my overshirt. We ambled up through the sycamore grove and round to the settlement. Wadi shared a shack with Nepthys. Dad and I lived in one of the brick houses higher up towards the temples. My lips were as tight as a tomb. I couldn't bring myself to tell her I was leaving.

Wadi kissed me on the cheek and ran the rest of the way to the shack. I stood and watched her until she reached her door safely. It was only then that I thought of the journey that lay ahead of me. Wars and trade deals had brought men of the Black Land to the borders of Mafkat, in the north, and Nubia, in the south, but never had anyone ventured into the heart of another country.

8

Harkhuf: The Journey Begins

We woke before dawn. The air was thick and already hot. Loading up the boats was painstaking, but with the help of the two soldiers who were coming with us, we got it done.

The effects of the wine had not fully worn off. I was in a playful mood. Everything seemed new and exciting but, at the same time, as if I had experienced it before. Once we reached the mainland, we had to leave the boats behind as the river was too narrow. We bought a caravan of donkeys at the local market and the farmer couldn't believe his luck. I had only one donkey to take charge of and I called him Greywacke because of his dark grey hide. We transferred our load, and, as we trailed our caravan along the river's edge, Seker hovered overhead. It wasn't long before I began to enjoy the wilderness. After our first full day of walking in the heat of the sun, we set up camp. I removed the cloth that had been protecting my head and wrung it out in the river, along with Dad's cap.

We had not travelled very far south of the border, and much of the landscape looked similar to the Black Land. I decided not to take it as a bad omen that we had spotted so many crocodiles and hippos wallowing in the shallow waters. They were said to embody the evil spirit of Set, who had murdered his own brother to gain power. People still believed that Set lurked in these parts, ready to come and get revenge on Horus, his nephew who defeated him. Yet it was Khnum, the god of the Iteru, who we were most concerned about, not forgetting his wife Satet, who controlled the flooding. I had seen how thin many of the islanders were in the days leading up to our departure. But I quickly ran out of energy for worrying. After I'd said my prayers, I lay down to sleep and went out like a lamp.

*

I woke to the sound of snorting. In the half-light, I saw that one of the donkeys had freed itself from its tether and was drinking from the Iteru. Tempted as it was to leave it and go back to sleep, I cast off my woollen blanket and tiptoed down to the bank so as not to wake the others.

As I approached the water, the snorting became a low whining. A murky shape hung in the pale waters.

44

I reached out to pat the donkey and heard the thud-thud of a crocodile. The donkey's front legs collapsed. Blood gushed from its neck, and I saw where viciously sharp teeth had pierced its flesh. Before I could act, the donkey's back legs thrashed and kicked as it was dragged under the water completely.

My muscles unfroze themselves. I ran back to the tents and beat the ground with my fists. The soldiers groaned. Dad's face emerged and he sniffed the air.

"Crocodiles—" I began.

"Search the undergrowth," Dad commanded.

One of the soldiers appeared and beat the reeds with sticks. A few monitors scurried out but nothing larger.

Satisfied that the area was clear, my father went about making a small fire.

"It's nearly dawn. Load up the donkeys," he said.

There was a loud shuffling as two more crocodiles lumbered down towards the water from higher up the bank. Where on earth had they been hiding? I jumped, nearly landing on one of their tails.

"There's another," called Midou, the slimmer of the two soldiers, pointing in the twilight.

My heart was thumping. Crocodiles don't waste time when they're hungry. Hasan, the larger soldier, smacked the earth with the full force of his body. I saw the crocodile move like a shadow in the opposite direction and released my breath. *What a close shave.*

A short while later, Dad took a pan and heated some dried beans with some river water. I pulled down our tents and gathered our belongings in neat piles. We had to move on, and fast.

"That first croc won't be far from its dinner," said Dad.

I tried to block the dead donkey out of my mind. Dad was angry with himself. I had seen him in moods like this before.

"You've got to head back to the island," he said. "I can't risk taking you any further."

I was crestfallen but also angry. Did he really think it was a good idea to send me back on my own?

"But ..."

"No buts, Harkhuf. This is too dangerous for a boy of your age."

I was fourteen, not a little boy. Did Dad think I was a coward? There was no use arguing with him.

The four of us ate our breakfast in silence. I cursed the river for its cruelty. It was hours before I could bring myself to talk to Dad again. He had given orders for Hasan to take me back to Elephantine Island. I packed up the last of my things whilst Hasan paced up and down the bank.

Greywacke was grazing. Dad cleaned out the pan in the river.

"You're good with the animals," he said levelly.

I said nothing, feeling that silence was still my most powerful tool. I hooked the straps of my bag around Greywacke's neck. He brayed softly, showing his affection. All the donkeys were grazing by now, chewing sparse patches of green and brown. Midou and Hasan were shaping branches into pointed sticks.

"Why are they making those?" I asked.

My father followed my line of gaze.

"You'll be less prone to attack," he said.

"I'm the least likely to be attacked," I blurted.

"By men, perhaps, but animals have less mercy."

"I was the one who saw the crocodile." I heard my tone begin to sound like begging.

47

"Perhaps, son, but do you really want to be out here in the wilderness when you could be back with your friends, enjoying the finer things in life?"

I tried to sound more in control. "Yes. Anyway, if the drought continues, there won't be many of the finer things left. We've got to do something."

"I said no, son. Now go and pack your things."

I headed over to where Midou and Hasan were sharpening the sticks. Dad was busy clearing up after breakfast. This was not one of our typical arguments. I led the remaining donkeys behind a thicket of bamboo. They didn't seem to notice as I waded into the river to drag their brother out, but I didn't have the strength to do it. It was like trying to pull a boulder. I took some rope and tied a knot to make a loop, which I wrapped around the wet beast's head. I could just about see what I was doing in the morning light. I trailed the other end of the rope up and over the bank, through the thicket and around the middle of our fittest donkey. It was Hasan's donkey. I was thankful that he wouldn't be able to see what came out the water as I lured him further towards the desert with some dried fruit.

Midou and Hasan came closer. Their eyes flickered and widened as they saw the grey mass being hauled along the sand. There wasn't much left of the carcass. I took out my pocket knife and gave it to Midou.

"Cut it up. We're going to need the meat," I said, looking him in the eye.

Midou put the sack he was carrying down on the ground. The job needed some serious physical strength, and although Hasan was larger than Midou, it was more fat than muscle. I thought Midou might refuse or, worse, ask to speak to Dad. Midou's face broke into a smile. He leaned down, and I looked away when I heard the knife plunge down. I don't like the sight of blood.

Hasan, who had been quietly taking it all in, laughed. Dad finished his prayers and began walking towards us. I stepped forward and walked to meet him halfway. Sighing, he put his hand on my shoulder.

"Thank you," he said. "We'll need the meat."

"That's what I thought." My voice sounded like it belonged to someone else.

He was pensive then. He looked as if he was thinking back, to some point in his past. A smile came to his lips. I was worried he was going to hug me.

"You've proven yourself, son. You don't have to go home if you don't want to. We need a thinking man like you."

Thinking man? Dad had never used either of those words to describe me before.

"I remember when that kid Nizam was giving you a hard time last year," he said. "It's difficult to remember being that age, when everything is still new and interesting. But the trouble is, no one believes in you when you're young. No one listens. Not properly. My own dad never listened to me. It used to make me so angry when he laughed at my plans to work for the pharaoh. We didn't get on at all. I want us to be different, do you understand?"

I looked at him and felt my lip tremble.

"Yes," I said. "You know I want this more than anything. To see the world."

"Perhaps you'll be able to make a living from it one day, son. Times change."

I nodded and felt myself changing too.

*

The cool morning air made the journey seem more bearable. We covered a good distance before the sun began to rise. First, it filled the sky with a gentle haze, and then it nearly blinded us with its brightness. We had spread the load across the other animals and they were slower now. Midou, like me, now only had one donkey to lead.

We kept close to the Iteru, but not too close. River folk called out to us. Their crops were failing, but the floods were often unpredictable. Like the sun, moon and sky, the floods inspired a sense of mystery and awe of the gods. Dad was in better spirits and entertained us with stories about Elephantine Island. He remembered with pride how he had wooed my mother in the early days. Mum, like many women on the island, had been a priestess of love. At festival time, the priestesses painted their lips with red ochre paint and their brows with lead. I thought back to Wadi's dance just days before and smiled to myself.

But now I was completely sober, something began to weigh on me. Wadi had no idea where I was. How could I have let this happen? She would never forgive me. I was starting to wonder if I should have gone back when I was given the opportunity. I composed letters to her in my head, explaining everything. I wasn't homesick, not at all. But already

51

the island seemed a long way away, a place of happy memories and very little trouble. Soon we would need to update the pharaoh on our progress. We had seen elephants, which – apart from their tusks – I had only seen in hieroglyphs, and the same strange horses that the chiefs had given to Pharaoh Merenra.

Seker had been circling above and returning to us every now and then to show she was tracking our path. The trees were thornier along this stretch of the Iteru. Nizam had once told me that in Nubia there was such a thing as a man-eating tree. It sounded like one of those stories people told children to make them squirm, but the truth was I had no idea what to expect once we crossed over the borderlands. If a crocodile could eat a human, who was to say that there wasn't a tree that could do the same? I thought of the pharaoh's amulets, which Dad had hidden at the bottom of a sack of dates. Surely they would ward off any danger?

*

It was on the fifth day that we found the campfire. Dusk hadn't quite fallen but we had already put up tents using thick sheets of papyrus and branches of acacia. We didn't bother with ground sheets as we were used to having insects crawling over us. It was a good spot. In the distance, we could see the gentle spurt of the second waterfall and the narrowing of the Iteru. Midou saw the strangers first. He made us hide behind a reed thicket. Three men were sitting around a large spit. They looked very different to the Nubians I had met in the Black Land. Their hair was longer and more ragged. Three spears were rammed into the sand next to them.

Greywacke snorted. Our cover was blown. The three men looked up at once, angry and menacing. One grabbed a spear and stepped towards us. Midou acted quickly. He held up his hands to show he had no weapon but this did not stop the shouting stranger, whose words I recognised to be Nubian. Midou's gesturing was useless. Dad dug around in the stores and pulled out one of the cloth wraps Midou had filled with donkey meat. He waved it in the air then pulled at the flaps of cloth, shouting words I didn't understand.

The men beckoned us nearer. I laughed with relief and nervousness. All four of us stepped towards the campfire. I thought they were going to kill us. We ate goat from the spit and my father broke open a small sack of figs. The bread we had brought was now stale but we shared what was left, mopping up the meat juices from our palm-leaf plates. I learned a few more Nubian words that evening. One of the men boasted that he had once killed a snake using just a rock and his bare hands. When Dad asked what it had tasted like, the Nubian frowned. Apparently it was not a delicacy. We each rinsed our plates in the river and put the damp leaves away in our bags. My bag was almost empty. I had brought a number of things to remind me of home and to help me stay prepared for the road ahead: a lock of my mother's hair, a small comb, a mirror and a knife for emergencies. The knife was quite new and sharp, so it would be useful for cutting fruit, meat and bread.

After we had stayed a decent amount of time and thanked the men for their hospitality, we wandered back to our camp, grateful for some rest. At dawn, the sound of Seker's unmistakable call could be heard. I whistled and she swooped down towards the water. The others were not in their tents. Blankets lay strewn across the ground. I looked around and saw that Dad was already down by the bank. I joined him and found he was writing a scroll to the pharaoh. I marvelled over the careful strokes made by the reed pen. I wished I could write so well. Tying the letter to Seker's leg, I whispered gently to her before she launched off into the skies.

I was keen to get moving again.

"Why did you change your mind about sending me home?" I asked.

"When a son attends his father, it is a twofold joy for both, as the old saying goes."

"You sound like grandma."

Dad coughed and then smiled. "Midou and Hasan have gone to investigate inland," he said. "There is no fishing along this stretch of the Iteru. It is not safe."

"Will we take the desert road?" I asked. I had visions of terrible thirst.

Dad gestured to the donkeys. "We can load these lazy beasts up with as much water as we need."

"Greywacke isn't lazy," I protested.

"You must stop naming every animal you come across, Harkhuf. It will ruin your appetite!"

Midou and Hasan soon returned with some fresh Nubian *shamsi*. I ate the bread slowly, savouring the taste. Would I ever experience such simple luxury again? I had missed my opportunity to write to Wadi. I imagined my arrival back on Elephantine Island.

Surely, she'll forgive me when she sees the exotic gifts I bring her.

9
Zau: Island Life

To His Excellency, Merenra Nemtyemsaf,
Day 5
We pray to Amun-Ra that the Black Land is safe.
The banks of the Iteru are dry to the second
waterfall, but we hope that the gods will smile on us
again. Crocodiles lurk everywhere but we have only
lost one donkey. We are heading east to the dunes
of Nubia, from where we will go further south to meet
the chiefs and lay the amulets.
Our most humble thanks for this great honour.
Iry and Harkhuf

*After I'd finished reading Harkhuf's scroll, I rolled it
up and closed the door to the new cage. I had seen
Seker flying north. A single whistle had brought her
to the ground. I moved the cage away from the
window, out of sight. I didn't plan to kill Seker. She
was too useful. Perhaps the pharaoh would send me
to find Iry and Harkhuf if the bird brought no news.
Then again, I had my own mission to complete now.*

So this was what the pharaoh had asked the island men to do: lay amulets for the gods to bring on the floods. Why was I never chosen for exciting missions? I had only been to the second waterfall on a boat-building trip. Oh, what am I worrying about. Harkhuf won't last long out there.

There's no point in taking the water reading as the river clearly isn't rising. Instead, I spend my days shooting arrows on the bank: a fitting exercise for the Land of the Bow. Mostly I down geese, but occasionally I catch bee-eaters, pheasants and laughing doves. I haven't told Wadi and the other girls how I get their feathers, which I give them as gifts, but they are always delighted. I eat the bird meat alone, after cooking the paltry flesh on a small fire. Down on the bank is my favourite place on the island, where I'm shielded from nosey neighbours by reeds and palm trees the size of obelisks.

I hate my new office. Dust has already coated the furniture and piles of papyrus have built up so quickly: letters (from the pharaoh, my own contacts and from Father), sheets containing my attempts at calculating tax, and records of Iry's water readings. I need an assistant but don't want anyone who would get on my nerves. I thought Wadi might be nice to have around. I asked her but she politely refused, saying she was too busy with her own work. Maybe I will need to use potions and spells to change her mind.

Gamal once taught me a love spell he had heard prescribed at the palace. You need to find nine apple pips and put them in a cup of your own urine. The urine part wasn't what disgusted me – it was the idea of kissing a girl. I learned a lot of heka-magic from Gamal. Then, later, I served as an apprentice to Seneni. That was when I wanted to become a priest. In some ways, Seneni has remained a mentor to me. He taught me about mana, the inner power we all possess, but more importantly, he showed me how to use it.

I'm not saying I can work miracles, but I wouldn't think twice about using my gift to get what I want. I have a good memory, so I can learn all the chants and incantations perfectly. Seneni said I'm a natural when it comes to heka, probably because of my reddish hair. His scrolls have been coming almost daily now. He sends his own messengers. Some of them are a real pain to get rid of. They expect to be treated as guests and I have to remind them that Elephantine Island isn't the City of the White Walls.

I think Seneni is getting nervous about the sacrifice. No wonder he needs my help. He writes a little bit about what's happening at the palace but mostly it's just nagging. "Remember to find some of Iry's personal belongings." "Find the blood of the youngest pup for the spell." Basic stuff, really. I just want to get the sacrifice done quickly so that the pharaoh, and that pathetic boy, will see what I'm made of.

10

Harkhuf: Striking Gold

The desert was never-ending. We didn't want to travel too far away from the water but were keen to explore what lay beyond the Iteru. The men who had eaten the donkey with us told us that there was a larger village within reach but that it would take us more than two days to get there on foot. They were right: the journey took three days. Dad blamed the donkeys for our slow progress, but I could see he was also exhausted. Mosquitoes fed hungrily on our limbs like suckling babies. We loaded the caravan with as many jugs of water as we could and drank regularly, but the heat was still unbearable.

We came across five or six Nubian women selling dried fruit and fish. With plenty of dates and figs in our own stores, we were only tempted by the fish, and ate it ravenously, trading it for bangles and beads. Dad questioned the women about Kerma, the city said to be at the heart of Nubia, but the language barrier seemed to be getting stronger. The women looked at him as if he were daft and giggled amongst themselves.

After the laughter had died down, an older lady pointed back towards the river.

"Setju," she said, rolling her hand as if to show a longer journey. "Setju, Kerma."

Dad didn't want to go back to the river. Nemeh had already warned us about that route and the sandstone cliffs looked like hard work. We hoped to find a village inland where we could replenish our supplies and begin our trail south-west again, heading straight for Kerma. Here we hoped to meet the most powerful Nubian chiefs. The women whispered and pointed as we headed off into the desert, but Dad paid no notice.

The first stirrings of civilisation were near to what looked like a quarry. The land was shaped with steps and craters and a few figures could be seen at the quarry's edge. I suggested heading straight over and introducing ourselves, but Dad was more cautious. He wanted to set up camp behind a dune to rest and plan our next move. Midou and Hasan were grateful for a break, as were the donkeys, who were beginning to show signs of wear and tear. Greywacke's hoofs were worn beyond measure, and all of us were suffering from leaky blisters. We didn't light a fire that night, but ate a basic meal of garlic,

stale bread and dates. Raw garlic isn't my favourite –
it makes me retch. It was enough to ward off our
hunger, but we were in dire need of a hot meal and
something more appetising to chew on.

We fed the pink bird and the snake and gave
them some water. They hadn't suffered the heat like
we had. But it would soon be bitterly cold. When
Dad had told me we were packing panther skins as
blankets, I laughed. I hadn't realised the desert at
night was colder than the morning river. Even with the
blankets my skin prickled at night, and the hair on my
arms stood up like the fur of a cat. The sky seemed
bigger with no temples or cliffs to block it out, and the
stars were the only reassurance that we had not fallen
off the edge of the earth.

*

The following morning, as we loaded our supplies
back onto the caravan, we saw the cluster of men
again at the entrance of what looked like a cave or
shaft. They all carried spears and their white
loincloths stood out against their skin. Each man
seemed to guard a different entrance.

"Carry the amulets in your *shendyt*," Dad told me.

"I don't think the gods will like that," I replied.

Dad wasn't in the mood for humour. As we emerged from behind the dune, we couldn't help feeling watched. We were only about a hundred cubits away when one of the men, the tallest one, attempted to speak to us. Dad greeted him in our own tongue, then in Nubian.

"We come in peace," he began.

The man stepped forward and stroked Greywacke's chest. I pointed to the chain around his neck, expressing my fascination, and he hit the ground with his spear. The other men moved in around us and inspected us closely, opening up some of the sacks on our load, perhaps to get a better idea of who we were.

None of us spoke. The men looked at us with a mixture of suspicion and amusement. The donkeys were led away and Dad looked pained, but I was still hopeful. As far as they knew, we had nothing of value and they wouldn't find anything in our stores. It was amazing that the pink bird and the viper had survived the journey, shielded from the sun by papyrus sheets and fed on insects we had found along the way. But these men didn't seem very interested in exotic wildlife. They were more interested in us.

The tall man paced up and down. I was starting to feel uneasy. Moments later, another man stepped forward and led Dad away to one of the cave entrances. He looked back at me with eyes as shrivelled as raisins. Before I could call out to him, I could feel myself being pulled in the opposite direction. I was thrust into the cave. I didn't even get a good look at my captor's face. Hours must have passed. All I remember is the cold hard ground of the cavern, my burning hunger and a scraping sound that bruised my ears.

A long while later, and after a disorienting sleep, a chink of daylight spilled into the cavern and I was confronted by a guard. He led me outside into the blinding light. Dad and the soldiers were nowhere to be seen. I considered making a run for it, but where would I go? I had no choice but to follow the guard as he strode round to the entrance of a shaft.

He clambered down a wooden ladder and I went after him. Young men were busying themselves with tools. This must have been the sound I had heard. I looked back up the shaft to see a tiny speck of light.

As my eyes adjusted to the darkness underground, I noticed that the walls around me were faintly shiny. *Gold.* None of the other workers paused to look at me. Then I saw why. Another guard stood guard with a whip, looking out for any slackers. He threw something heavy down next to my feet: a chisel. What was I supposed to do with a chisel? I was starting to panic. Did anyone speak my language? Would they believe I had been sent by the pharaoh? Would they even care?

As my mind whirred with questions, I began to chip away at the rock and before long I had created a small mound of rubble. My arm was heavy with the labour. My head was numb. I heard a clanging noise and the other workers began to leave their piles of gold behind them. They formed a queue, which I joined, and one by one we climbed up another ladder. About two cubits above was a small clearing, lit with oil lamps. On a stone slab, some bread and beer were laid out. I chewed at a piece of hard bread and slumped against the wall. There was just a dirty pit for us to relieve ourselves in. The smell made me gag. I felt feral – unwashed and desperate. There were holes in my vision, big black patches. What had they done with Dad?

11

Harkhuf: The Red Land

After my seventh cold and restless night, I woke to find one of the guards writing notes on a piece of papyrus. In the pale light, I could just make out a smile on his face. Our eyes met and he nodded at me, gesturing that I should get up and get back to work. Most of the others were still asleep. I hadn't been able to tell if they were my age or younger. Some of them seemed to enjoy the labour. They would sigh with accomplishment when slabs of rock and gold fell to the ground. But not me – I could find no satisfaction in a task I hadn't chosen to do.

I found a way to keep some of the smaller nuggets cupped in one hand as I worked, and I started to memorise the layout of the mine. At the latrine, I stowed them in the pouch hidden in my *shendyt*. It seemed like fair payment for the work I had done. Besides, I would need something to barter with if I ever managed to get out. I couldn't stop thinking about Wadi. My lungs were heavy and I was weaker than I ever had been.

That night, as I lay under my blanket staring at the darkness, I heard a whistle. Looking up, I saw one of the guards, his face partly lit by daylight. He gestured for me to come nearer. They would cut off my hands if they realised I had been stealing. I threw off my blanket and shimmied up the ladder after the guard, out into the dazzling light. There in the quarry yard, I saw our serpent and the pink bird in their cages. The guard pressed a pouch into the palm of my hand. I opened it to find about double the amount of gold I had already taken. *Is this a trick? Will they search me?* I tried to breathe normally. The guard pointed again to the snake and the bird and I finally understood that they were buying the exotic creatures after all.

I was just beginning to wonder if they had realised their mistake in keeping me at the mine, when another guard brought Greywacke round to the front. I had never been happier to see a donkey in my life. Most of my sacks were still on him and I was pleased to see that he had been loaded with fresh jugs of water, loaves of bread and crates of fish, already swarming with flies. The guard smiled and ushered me away. Was I being released? Or led somewhere else? Perhaps Dad had already been freed. I decided to head towards the river. It would take me days to reach it but I took my chances and led Greywacke towards the baking desert.

*

I nearly lost my mind on that two-day trek without human company. I could only think of the worst possible situations: about Dad, about Wadi, about Seker. Greywacke gave me some comfort and I began to talk to him as if he were a friend. On the first night, I didn't use a tent. Sleeping next to Greywacke, we were lucky we weren't taken for dead by vultures. The fish and bread restored my strength, but the desert air was as dusty as the mine and did nothing to ease my aching lungs.

Travelling had begun to take its toll on my body. My stomach was constantly upset and nausea prevented me from thinking clearly. It required all the focus I could muster just to put one foot in front of the other. Yet even when I tried to block out my thoughts, they would crowd my mind like echoes.

Being alone gradually became easier. I could walk at my own pace and I didn't have to fit in with the shifting moods of grown men. Preparing food became somehow more spiritual. I felt connected to the gods. Each meal I ate I felt I had earned. I prayed earnestly. It kept me focused on survival. My feet were throbbing and my vision was stained yellow, like old scrolls.

By the time I reached the river, I had forgotten what it was to feel clean. I tethered Greywacke and began to untie the load on his back, finding two sacks of hay in the process that seemed to cheer him up. His hoofs had healed, but my own feet were beyond repair. I peeled off the linen that I had wrapped around my blisters and saw the red and yellow mess underneath. Tearing off my *shendyt,* I placed the pouches of amulets and gold in the bottom of one of the hay sacks and ran into the Iteru. I didn't look to see who might be watching as I waded out into the shallow waters, forgetting all about the threat of crocodiles and hippos.

My feet stung but, luckily, I had packed a spare *shendyt* and bandages. The fresh, clean cloth felt good. It was only then that I looked around properly. In and amongst the cliffs, there were several tiny beaches of sand like the one I stood upon. On one of them, stalls had been set up. A group of women were milling about. Energised from my swim, I headed over in the hope that they might have seen a slightly bald old man.

A slender Nubian girl offered me some fruit, which had been stewed beyond recognition. Young boys were playing drums and pipes and I joined in with the dancing. I could feel the midges and mosquitoes feasting on my legs and ankles but I didn't care. It was the most fun I'd had since the Festival of Wag! The music was so different to ours. It sounded like birdsong. The drums were not too loud either. It was late afternoon and the sun had cooled off slightly. I looked around me at the unspoilt river. It was fuller than on the island. Had rain fallen whilst I had been in the mine?

*

I had forgotten most of my troubles by the time I got back to where Greywacke was tethered. There I found Midou helping himself to my stores. We embraced and it felt good to be able to have a conversation using words instead of gestures.

"What happened?" I asked. "Where are the others?"

"I haven't seen them since we got to the mine."

He broke eye contact and gnawed on a roll.

"Why did they let you go?" I asked, rummaging for some dried fruit.

Midou shrugged, mid-chew.

"How did you get here?" I asked, still full of questions.

"One of the men led me here underground—"

I spat out the date in my mouth. "What?"

"Their tunnels go all the way to the sea," Midou continued. "The Red Sea, that is. There are three mines in the complex, and we're very near to another one."

It was called the Red Sea because no pharaoh would ever send an army there, not unless he wanted to lose every single soldier.

"Let me get this right," I said. "My dad could be anywhere between here and the Red Sea?"

Midou nodded. None of it made any sense. What did the Nubians want with tunnels? Midou's facial expressions told me there was something else he wanted to say. Did he know something I didn't?

My skull felt pinched, as if my brains were being pulled by an embalmer's hook. It was never going to be an easy friendship between us. We had to get to Kerma. *Forward not backward*, as Dad used to say.

12

Zau: Hide and Seker

Nothing has really changed on the island since I moved here, although little Nizam is becoming quite an ally. He helped persuade Wadi that there is more to life than pottery and painting. She came for an interview last week and the thought came into my head that she wouldn't make the worst wife in the world. I don't know what came over me. More than anything, I need some help keeping the office looking presentable. If the pharaoh visits for any reason, I will have a lot of explaining to do.

Wadi started work two days ago, which is motivating in some ways. She knows how to keep the office tidy and quickly learned I don't like idle chatter. Villagers are beginning to ask questions about the drought and about Iry and Harkhuf. I told Wadi to let them know that they were in the capital city, working on the pharaoh's tomb. When I first told her, she didn't believe me, but gradually her eyes became sad and she stopped talking about them. I waited until she had gone out to eat her lunch before I forged the scroll.

Once I had made a copy of the royal seal, I rolled up the scroll and released Seker. Her shrieking was unbearable but within moments, she was flying south as instructed.

Nizam's dad has closed the bakery to the public. There's just not enough grain to feed everyone. Of course, he still makes me a few loaves each week. Nizam usually brings them over to me. I actually invited him to shoot with me a couple of times. He has a terrible aim but at least he's keen. He'll need to learn to shoot properly if this drought carries on much longer. I've thought about giving lessons to all the island men but then there would be less meat for me. I've already noticed less birds flying around these parts. Still, if I get really desperate, I could always give Seker a try. I've never tasted falcon meat before.

Yesterday, as I was hunting on the beach, Wadi's sister Nepthys approached me. I had already gathered a pile of small birds. No doubt she expected me to share them.

The air was murderously hot.

"Supplies are running low in the temple," she called, spying the birds.

Only days ago, I had seen Nepthys bathing Thutma, Nizam's mum. Thutma used to be a very large woman and was now reduced to skin and bones. Hunger had driven some of the younger men half mad, but it was the older population that was getting sick.

Nepthys's cough reminded me that she was expecting a response.

"I'll do what I can, of course."

I spent the afternoon deboning my catch. The birds were small but I had enough meat for a stew. I fell asleep whilst it simmered and woke up just as the sun was setting. Through the reeds I could see the last boats and rafts of the day passing by. I was beginning to wonder if my plans would unfold as hoped. I might be stuck on the island forever. Reaching for my glass of wine, I tried to put these thoughts out of my mind. Failure isn't an option, I told myself.

13

Harkhuf: The Kingdom of Kerma

Midou and I set out on the river route to Kerma, where I hoped to meet with the Nubian chiefs again. We began skinning and cooking our own food: goats when we could find them, poultry, jerboas and spiny mice. I disliked eating the mice as they always reminded me of a story my dad told me when I was a child called "The Mouse as Vizier". It was a stupid story really, but I loved it and made him tell it over and over again. I don't know how he had the energy after a full day's work.

The funny thing is that Midou had never heard that story. I managed to spare enough saliva to tell it to him as I remembered it. The little mouse solved a riddle and became vizier, but the punishments he gave were too severe and so the pharaoh banished all mice underground. I told it like a proper bedtime story though, adding in all the details about the other animals.

"I'll tell that one to my child," he said.

We didn't talk much – we had to save our energy – but I found out that he had grown up somewhere between Elephantine Island and the White Walls. He told me he has four brothers, which made me envious. Being an only child can be – well – lonely.

A few days into our journey, Seker hovered above us. I stopped in my tracks. A scroll landed at our feet and Seker landed soon afterwards with a thud. Moments later, Midou asked me what was wrong. I hadn't realised I was shaking.

Day 16
Iry and Harkhuf,
How careless of you to lose a donkey. By now you must have been disbanded and robbed! The Black Land awaits your return before the people starve. I expect to hear better news soon. If not, I may be forced to send replacements to lead the mission.
His Excellency,
Pharaoh Merenra

"Can I read it?" asked Midou. I passed him the scroll and he scratched his head.

"It was written in haste. I wouldn't worry too much about it," said Midou.

I was grateful for Midou's moral support, but he didn't know the true nature of the mission. How long would it be before I finally gave in and confided in him? I had to respond. I had to write to Wadi. I checked Greywacke's load for any writing materials but found none. We passed the rest of the journey in silence, each of us gathering our own thoughts. We fell into a rhythm, stopping every hour or so to drink. In the middle of the day, we set up tents to rest from the intense heat. Our lunch consisted of rotting fish and stale bread.

It took us two and a half days to finally reach Kerma. I thought it was a mirage at first. The kingdom was impressive. The sheer scale of it was enough to make me feel about as significant as an ant. We stopped in the shade of the outer walls. Guards were dotted around. Would we be turned away? I reached into the sack that now contained my pouch. A few nuggets of gold bought our entry. Once inside the walls, the city was heaving. Men and women ferried sacks to and fro on their heads. Just within sight was the busy blur of what could only have been a market. It wouldn't be long until I could put pen to papyrus.

It was easy to get distracted. There was red and black pottery for sale as well as freshly speared and roasted gazelle. Elderly stallholders withered in the shade. Finally I saw reed pens. They were nestled on a stall selling rock carvings of small animals. I held out the smallest nugget of gold I carried with me. The stallholder beamed and put it in a pouch for safekeeping. He gestured for me to take my pick. I chose the smallest pen and picked out a carving of a cat for Wadi.

A familiar voice echoed around the marketplace. I turned to see Nemeh, the Nubian I had met with the pharaoh. He was striding towards me with arms outstretched. We embraced and, once I had introduced Midou, Nemeh led us away to a tall structure that he called the *defuffa*. At first glance, it would have been easy to mistake the place for a natural outcrop, shaped by the gods of creation. But closer inspection showed that it was human hands that had sculpted the rock. My jaw must have been hanging low. Nemeh laughed. Midou and I murmured sounds of appreciation and awe. Inside, more familiar faces were gathered. There was a meeting taking place.

On seeing us, the elder chiefs called an end to proceedings. All three of us bowed before the eldest chief, and Nemeh signalled for me to step forward. Greywacke was tethered outside. I had taken the Pharaoh's offerings from his load and decided to start with the most impressive gifts. I was suddenly nervous. How had I stepped into my dad's sandals like this? I had never imagined dealing directly with the Nubian chiefs myself. I presented a few emeralds in the palm of my trembling hand. The jewels glistened amongst the gold pieces, and the eldest chief cried out. My second offering was one of Wadi's faience pots and a statue that I had forgotten I had even brought with me. Wadi's talents were not lost on the Nubians.

Midou and I were presented with a feast. There was no shortage of food and we filled our empty stomachs with more delicious *shamsi* bread. We were given round, brightly coloured fruits that were at once sweet and bitter. Nemeh offered us dried fish and ostrich eggs. We were so involved in eating that we forgot all about our sore feet.

That night, Midou and I were given quarters to share. I was unable to sleep. I still had to write scrolls to Wadi and the pharaoh. I crept outside and sat on the step leading up to our room. The stars, cradled in the sky, bathed the kingdom in an exquisite light. Stray cats and dogs roamed the streets looking for scraps. I wrote quickly but from the heart, deciding not to tell the pharaoh that Dad was missing. I would give the scrolls to Seker in the morning.

14

Zau: Charity

To His Excellency, Merenra Nemtyemsaf
Day 30
I know you are disappointed, dear pharaoh. The chiefs of Kerma are delighted with your gifts. It won't be long before we find the source of the Iteru and the floods return again. All will be well.
May your heart weigh heavily in the passage to Duat.
Your humble Iry and Harkhuf

So, Harkhuf fancies himself as an explorer, does he? Ha ha. I've got a right mind to tell the islanders what's really going on and to announce Harkhuf's death. He'll never make it back. No, he won't survive the heat, let alone the Nubians.

And what's all this about the source of the Iteru? Surely the pharaoh doesn't think the gods will be fobbed off with a few amulets? If the people of the Black Land spent less time complaining about stomach aches and more time praying to Khnum and Satet then the drought would be lifted. Luckily

Hasan has arrived safely back on the island without being seen. He reckons Harkhuf has a couple of days left to live at most. He's been turned out into the desert with just a crate of fish to keep him going. Hasan saw it with his own eyes! What Iry and Harkhuf don't realise is that Hasan speaks Nubian. He was able to bribe the guards at the mine in no time. They were pleased that they were being paid to have another slave. Hasan came straight back to the island to let me know Iry had been captured. No-one will suspect a thing.

I don't know why Seneni didn't tell me anything about this "mission" into Nubia, especially since it was actually Seneni's idea to capture Iry. As far as priests go, Seneni is pretty strange, it's got to be said. He rarely speaks, and when he does it's with the urgency of a mother warning a child. He's paying me handsomely though, so I won't complain.

As a sacrifice, Iry is ideal. He might be old, but his powers are still strong and the pharaoh needs all the help he can get making it to the Kingdom of Duat in the afterlife. True, it would take more than a concoction of dog's blood to purify his soul, but he doesn't really go in for devouring human flesh like the pharaohs before him. Not that I really care what happens to him. I just want my fee and I wouldn't mind seeing the back of Iry and his son too. It was lucky I met with Hasan when I did, or the whole plan would have been impossible. The trouble with Pharaoh Merenra is he doesn't know what's good for him.

Iry is being kept at the mine for the time being, until we can figure out a way to get him prepared for the offering. No doubt they will put him to good use. I just hope he doesn't drop down dead from natural causes before I lay eyes on him again.

The islanders are becoming more and more irritating. Wadi didn't show up for work this afternoon. Rumour has it she's not well. Everybody says her ribs are protruding from her flesh. Something she ate has made her sick and now she can't stomach anything. Her busybody sister Nepthys is nursing her as well as a load of other weak-spirited souls that gather daily at the temple, begging for charity. Nepthys nags me constantly. "Can you help with feeding the sick?" "Will you call a ritual priest?" Nepthys is such a shrew. I hate the way her nose wiggles when she talks and the hair on her face looks like whiskers. She had the cheek to come and see me again. She has no right setting foot on the governor's beach. I am entitled to a little privacy, am I not? I told her if she came again I'd put her in prison. The funny thing is she thought I was joking.

It's not just Wadi that's sick. The temple is overflowing with invalids. I have hardly left my beach for days and have taken to sleeping there as it's the one place on the island that is off-limits to peasants. I'm getting tired of waiting for Seneni to write back to my last scroll. He's gone very quiet. I really hope the pharaoh hasn't found us out.

15
Harkhuf: Bes

Our first full day in Kerma made me question everything. Nemeh had been sent to make sure we were comfortable and had everything we needed. He appeared just before sunrise, bringing two cups of tea with him. The smell was peculiar, almost medicinal. Midou and I drank gratefully, both of us eager not to upset our hosts. Breakfast awaited us in the *defuffa*. The meal was not as grand as the previous day's spread, but two helpings of ostrich eggs and bread was enough to restore my strength. Nemeh was full of energy. He enjoyed the attention we received as we walked around the kingdom. No efforts were made to hide the disbelief at our appearance. The longest stares were from the elderly residents. They spent most of their time sitting on chairs in the shade, fanning away flies and chewing on stalks.

The tour of Kerma lasted several hours. We were shown boats, fishing tools, bakeries, temples and family homes. In the afternoon, we spent time with the local boys, playing ball games on the dusty plains. I couldn't imagine going back to the desert. Nemeh said we would meet the big chiefs the following day. The way we were treated made it all worthwhile: the exhaustion, the time at the mine, the anguish over my dad. I was finally growing up. I think Dad would be proud.

It was on our third day in Kerma that Nemeh introduced us to Bes. After yet another delicious breakfast, Nemeh led us into the desert. We arrived at the entrance to a small cavern just as the sun was making its appearance over the horizon. Nemeh burrowed his head inside the narrow opening and whistled loudly. A tiny man pushed passed Nemeh's legs, looking unhappy to have been disturbed so early in the morning. He wiped some crumbs from his mouth and then, much to our amazement, spoke in a familiar language.

"I suppose I should introduce myself. I'm Bes," he said, suddenly more alert.

Nemeh left us alone with the pygmy. I was still speechless but I made an effort to recover my tongue.

"Are you from the Black Land?" I ventured.

"I have never been there," Bes told us. "But the chiefs have often brought me texts to decipher. Usually pretty boring stuff – trade, tax, that sort of thing. I prefer the holy texts."

"Right," I said. "So you're a priest, or ...?"

"I'm a scorpion charmer."

Dad had talked about scorpion charmers but I hadn't realise they actually existed.

"We got into a bit of trouble just north of here – in the desert," I said.

"At the mines?" asked Bes.

"Yes."

Midou was unnaturally quiet.

"The mines are run by the Medjay," explained Bes. "Their leader is not the same as here in Kerma."

"Do they use ... slaves?" I asked, fearful that Dad's fate had been sealed.

"You could say that. Have you lost someone?"

"My father," I admitted.

His expression changed to one I could not read. I was beginning to think I would need to let all of Kerma know the true nature of my mission. How else would we find the true source of the Iteru?

"The river is much wider here than where we are from," I continued.

Bes frowned. "It is usually even wider, but this year we have had less water. It is the first time in living memory that the water level has been so low."

"Are you worried?"

"I never worry. I leave that to the experts."

"What do you think the chiefs will do?" I asked.

"What can they do? In Kerma, we believe that the gods fight amongst themselves."

"They don't seek to punish us?"

"What do you mean?"

I drew an image of Khnum, the god of the Iteru. "This is our river god," I explained. "He has the power to give, but he also takes lives. He wants to be adored."

Bes seemed to understand.

"Do you know where the river begins? Can you take us there?" I asked.

"Ah, where the two rivers meet?"

Two rivers? I was baffled. My father had only talked of the Iteru. I had no knowledge of any other river.

"Yes. It is a long way from here. At least a week on foot."

"Do you know the route?" I asked.

"It's all up here," he said, tapping his head. "I come from further south myself, not far from there."

"Now that is a happy coincidence," I said. "Will you come with us?"

Bes looked up at me.

"If you want to borrow me for your travels, we had better go to the *defuffa* and ask the chiefs. I think they will spare me, especially if you are able to bring the floods back."

My words were muffled by the sound of Seker's wings making their descent.

"A sacred falcon?" Bes seemed impressed.

"She has brought a reply from the pharaoh," I explained.

"So you can write? You may be of some use yet, young man."

"Anything we can do to help, just ask."

I unfurled the scroll and read:

Day 55
Dear Harkhuf,
This is your final chance. Prayers remain unanswered. Sickness and starvation is all around. If the floods do not arrive in the next week, you must return to Elephantine Island.
Pharaoh Merenra

"Do you mind if I read it?" asked Bes with a hint of mischief in his voice.

I hesitated. I couldn't allow Bes to read my correspondence with the pharaoh, and yet I understood perfectly his curiosity about our written language.

"I can't let you read it," I said. "But I can teach you how to write hieroglyphs."

16

Zau: Sickening for Something

Day 60
Wadi,
I could not find the words to tell you of our journey. I didn't want you to worry, but now I realise that to say nothing was far worse. You were right – I was born to discover. I will bring back tales of my travels and my mission. Until then, I ask that you don't forget me and that you can begin to forgive me.
Your eternal friend,
Harkhuf

I decided I should pay Wadi a visit. As she still hadn't come into the office, it seemed right to check that she really was ill. I wasn't about to give her Harkhuf's scroll though. She was propped up in her bed and seemed glad to see me. I hope she didn't get the wrong impression. She told me she was feeling slightly better. The pain in her stomach had gone. She was thirsty but said the thought of drinking the river water made her retch.

Next to her lay a pile of dried figs. She bit down on to one of them and chewed slowly as she spoke. Her stomach gurgled and I thought she was going to vomit. She swallowed loudly, thrust her weight forward onto her hips and swivelled round to the edge of the bed. I couldn't believe how thin she was. I made my excuses and told her if she saw her sister to remind her she was not to go near the beach again. Wadi had been unlucky, that was all. What was everyone getting so worked up about? Didn't they know it was best to stew food before you ate it?

I was curious to know why Wadi thought Harkhuf was such a born adventurer. I wanted to have a little fun and so, before I left, I asked her about what it was like growing up on the island.

"We used to play all day," she said. "We didn't have much work to do and so we'd go out catching butterflies or playing Find the Pharaoh. We made our own fun. Harkhuf was always coming up with new games."

Catching butterflies?! I had to stop myself from laughing out loud. These kids want to be taken seriously and they spend their time chasing butterflies?

17

Harkhuf: Where the Two Rivers Meet

With Bes happily saddled on top of Greywacke, we took the river route for part of the way then veered east into the desert to take a shortcut to the fourth waterfall. From there, we would need to make an even longer trek across the blistering sands before heading south to where the two rivers join. Bes assured us that we would be able to stock up on supplies at various points along the river. Somehow, I had forgotten how intense the heat could be.

When we finally reached the fourth waterfall, drenched in sweat, we arrived at a settlement that Bes called Napat. It was nowhere near as grand as Kerma, just a few mud brick houses along the river's edge. Bes spoke to the locals there who insisted that we slept in the shell of a house that was being built. There was no market to be seen, just the supplies that the families had from their own work on the land.

Midou was growing tired. I could sense he was missing home. He had told me about his wife back in the Black Land. She was expecting their first child, and he was worried that he wouldn't be back in time for the birth. I couldn't afford to lose him at this crucial stage of the journey. The truth was I needed his protection.

The desert was kind to us in the morning light. We were determined to make the crossing as swiftly as possible. Bes's light-hearted conversation took our minds off the long journey. Without it, the hours would have stretched into eternity. *Would you rather be a donkey or a fish?* Even Midou began to enjoy himself.

I asked Bes about the man-eating tree and he said it was nonsense. He did introduce us to the punt tree though. Its resin is sticky and watery at the same time. It shimmered as though it contained a thousand tiny suns, and in a way it did. It's amazing that any plants and trees can grow out there. Bes called the resin "heknu oil". He said it contained special properties for praising the gods. I was keen to tap as much of the oil as I could, as this was the sort of thing the pharaoh would want me to bring back. Every time we passed a punt tree, I used my knife to drain as much as I could from the bark and let it drip, drop by drop, into one of the vials that I had in my stores. Midou and I used small amounts to cover our blisters.

The smell was overpowering, like dried lemon peel mixed with smoke.

After three days of being back on my feet, my legs were starting to seize up. I glanced back and saw a shadow following close behind us. As it moved closer, the light dimmed and a cold wind picked up.

"Duck!" called Bes.

We threw ourselves on the hot desert floor, shielding our eyes and faces from the flying sand. Greywacke groaned and collapsed. Water fell from above, drenching our bodies as sand whipped around our faces. I pulled off my cloth cap and breathed through the thick cotton threads. The sand cut my face. Then the light and the heat returned in all their intensity. Our path was clear again.

"What in Khnum's name was that?" I asked.

"A desert warrior," said Bes.

The skies were attacking us, but they had brought us water – only the tiniest amount, but it gave me hope.

*

Greywacke didn't make it. I don't know how he died but maybe it was the shock of the sandstorm. I was numb. I kept reminding myself of what my dad had said about naming animals. Was it ridiculous to be so attached to a donkey? Some of my friends had cried when their cat died so I knew it wasn't just me. I could hear Dad's voice in my head telling me not to be so soft and to focus on the mission in hand.

After three days of walking and sleeping under the stars, we finally reached the river join. We were surrounded by swampland. I felt I would sink into the ground with every step. I was so close to completing the mission, but where exactly was I supposed to lay the amulets? I had not been given specific instructions. I couldn't just throw them into the river. There had to be some ceremony to it surely? I was in charge. I couldn't ask Bes or Midou. After so many years of wanting more responsibility and more choice, I began to see why adults were sometimes so bad at it.

As we curved around the east bank, I could see more of where the two rivers joined. It was unimaginably wide. Nubians were gathered at the edges, filling jugs and buckets of water to load onto their donkeys. At the widest point, settled in the green waters, was an island no bigger than the temple of Khnum.

"Nebu Island," said Bes. "It's sacred here. No one is allowed to set foot on it."

My heart sank. This must be the place for the offering.

"Not even if they are respectful?" I asked.

"Not even then. Unless you are on some kind of divine mission...?" He had that mischievous tone again. "But if any Nubians see you crossing over there, they will put an arrow in your backside."

"Well, then we must go at night."

"If you get caught, we don't know each other," said Bes.

Midou made a shelter to give us some shade.

As it got nearer to sundown, the Nubians finally began to disappear. I waded into the water. It was shallow enough to walk through.

"Midou, you stand guard," I said.

Midou took off his sandals and dipped his toes in the water. Bes stayed rooted to the spot. He appeared to be whittling down a reed to make a pen, but this was no time for writing memoirs. As I reached the island, I saw the reeds were overgrown. Bes had my knife, so I beat a path for myself using a large branch. I wasn't sure exactly what I was looking for, but I hoped it would soon become clear. After forty cubits or so, I found a nesting ibis. She turned to face a large tree. Its oversized roots jutted out above the ground like the ridges on a woman's neck and each of its leaves were the size of my hand. There were thousands of them. As I got closer, I could see that the bark had an unusual texture, like embroidered cloth. Had somebody carved into the tree?

On closer inspection, I noticed that the tiny markings were all natural. Tiny ripples like water-glyphs ran horizontally across the trunk. There was a rustling sound above me. I looked up to see a family of wild monkeys moving around in the tree. They were agitated. There was a high-pitched screaming sound as I loosened the fastening of my pouch. I tipped the remaining emeralds and gold nuggets into my hand, turning them over rapidly with my fingers.

The monkeys descended, too many to count. They held out their hands as if mimicking me. I placed a precious pellet in each of their outstretched palms. Then they clambered, one by one, to hide amongst the branches. At last, their shrieking died down and a sense of complete calm came over me. I checked the pouch. The wooden ankh was still at the bottom. I removed it carefully and placed it at the base of the tree. From above, I felt a mist engulf me. *Rain!*

18

Harkhuf: Return from Kerma

The river's renewal was gentle at first. In fact, it was barely noticeable unless you had seen the rain, which the people of the Black Land certainly wouldn't have. There was no point writing to the pharaoh, who would be informed of the rising water level by Zau. I hadn't seen Seker in weeks. As for Dad, I was hoping he had somehow made it back to the island. I was ready to celebrate, and Bes was keen to get back to Kerma to receive his share of the glory. I couldn't have done it without him. He told me there was much more to Kerma than I'd had time to see. He had a way of making things sound mysterious.

We retraced our route, swigging endlessly at the fresh rainwater that Midou had collected. Before long, my stomach eased and I began to feel well again. The people of Kerma seemed unaware of any changes in the river. Nemeh was surprised to see us, but as pleased as ever. Horus only knows what he thought of us. By now, Midou and I were completely unshaven. The three of us – Midou, Bes and me – were scrubbed, pummelled and polished. My wounds were dressed with resin and fresh bandages. A Nubian barber shaved our heads and faces. Nemeh gave me a mirror. The difference in colour between my temple and my cheeks was laughable.

"Monkey boy," Bes shrieked, unable to contain himself.

I took the jibes in good humour. He was a friend after all. I had the feeling things could only get better. I was beginning to allow myself to imagine seeing Wadi and even Dad. Part of me wanted to skip the return journey and wake up to find myself already back in the island, but I reminded myself that meeting new people and exploring Kerma was all part of the adventure. I had a dilemma though. If we took the same route back, there was a chance we would find Dad at the mine, but it would be risky. What if we were captured again? If we took a different route, we would be safer, perhaps, and there would be new scenery, maybe even new settlements. I had the wildest notion to take Bes back with us.

When I approached him, Midou in tow, he was dusting out his cave. He was very house-proud for someone who lived in nature.

"Are you ready for another journey?" I asked

"To the Black Land? I'm flattered, Harkhuf, really, flattered and honoured that you would have me as your guest."

I pictured the locals' faces on meeting Bes. They would make no secret of their surprise.

"I'll make a deal with you," Bes continued. "If you ever return to Kerma, I will join you again on your travels."

"What did you want to show me?" I asked, remembering Bes's cryptic words on the way back from Nebu Island.

"Oh, just the tunnels," he said.

Midou, who had been quietly examining his fingernails, looked up.

Bes explained. "They are getting old now they're crumbling all over the place. My size gives me some advantage. Sometimes it's like trying to fit an elephant in a burrow, but when I worked for the miners I sped along the passages, no problem."

"Why didn't you tell me you worked for the miners?" I asked.

Bes looked amused. "You didn't ask. I told you, I'm a scorpion charmer. Who do you think has the most trouble with scorpions round here? Yes, the miners! It's cool underground. The workers are more productive when they're not full of poison."

I looked at my feet. The new sandals Nemeh had given me were already dusty. My legs could walk for thousands of cubits, but it only took one man to open my mind to a whole new world of possibilities.

"Do you want to see for yourself?" Bes asked.

The whole thing was ridiculous. How could people crawl for such long distances?

"I don't want to go back to the mine," I replied, surprising myself with the depth my voice.

"There are other routes. You can go north and avoid the mine complex. You wouldn't get past the guards anyway."

"What about the donkeys? Do you use carts instead?" I asked.

"Don't worry about all that now. Just take a look inside, go for a wander. I checked for snakes this morning so you should be fine."

Bes led me through his home and towards the back of his living room. The tunnel was not marked, and any signs of crumbling had been removed. The inside walls looked smooth and cold. A small lamp had been lit and Bes passed me a torch. Once burning, it gave enough light for me to see about two cubits ahead of me, maybe more once my eyes adjusted. Midou sat on the ground in Bes's cave. He looked like a giant, but at least he was no longer stooping. It was my turn to lower my head as I stepped into the tunnel. Bes popped his head in after me.

"Boo!" he shouted and the echo made me start. I stepped forward a few paces, pleasantly surprised by the temperature. I remembered the mine and the relentless rhythm of chisel against rock. The walls of the tunnel were lighter in colour, and there was not a nugget to be seen, but something about being underground made my head feel heavy. I stopped, turned around and called back: "I'm not sure I'll last more than a day in here."

*

I wasn't sure about the tunnels but my skin was cracked and burnt from our days in the desert. Besides, it was something new. We left Bes for the time being and spent one more night in Kerma, before stocking up for our journey underground. We bought a couple of ostriches in the hope they would survive at least part of the journey back. Those eggs are feasts in themselves. Bes cleaned out the shells of several dozen and filled them from the trickle of water that had begun in the Iteru. In the market, I also saw jewellery made out of ostrich shells and bought a small necklace for Wadi.

Bes told us about the standing stones. He said when we reached them, he reckoned we should be about half-way back to Elephantine Island. He warned us that the tunnels would be just as tough as the desert. I knew I would miss his words of wisdom. He was right about the tunnels, that's for sure. Although there was no sun burning our faces, dragging carts all day wasn't kind to the spine. By the time we reached the end of the tunnel, the lamps were nearly out. We had no idea how long we had been underground. My eyes stung as my head emerged into the daylight like a snail from its shell.

There was nothing left of my supplies apart from some broken ostrich shell, which I left on the sand. One of the ostriches was just about alive. The other had died and we had done our best to wrap it up, but the stench was not pleasant. We left our carts by the mouth of the tunnel and walk a few cubits out into the cold desert night.

It didn't take us long to spot the standing stones. They were rocks, really. Great big slabs of rock. We could see a few men sitting next to them but they were so still that I began to wonder if they were actually men at all. As we got closer, I saw that they were barefoot and each of them had their eyes closed. They wore their beards long, and it became clear that they were all old enough to be my great-grandfathers – or even Midou's great-grandfathers. Their hair was mostly grey, and their skin dark and dry. We stopped and looked a bit longer, not wanting to disturb them from whatever it was they were doing. Midou looked tired.

"What are we going to offer them?" he asked.

I hadn't even thought about that. Bes had said the standing stones were abandoned. We weren't expecting company. Were these men guarding the stones? The Beards – as I chose to call them – did not seem threatening, but that's what I had thought about the men at the mine. I began to think about how we appeared to them. We hadn't washed in days. My stomach was turning over like a dying fish. Little stars danced in front of my eyes. We needed their help before we died of thirst.

One of the Beards must have heard Midou talking. I saw his eyes open – just a crack – then close again, the way a lizard's do. I shuffled back towards the tunnel and grabbed the pouch of gold.

"I thought you were keeping that somewhere safe?" said Midou. "It's all we have."

"Yes," I said, realising my own carelessness. I approached the Beards and crouched down by one of them. The Beard kept his eyes shut but he knew I was there. His face twitched as I spoke.

"Hello," I said.

The Beard's eyes opened but he remained still. His breathing told me he was unsure about me. I held out my hand to shake his but he just looked at it. I delved my fingers into the pouch of gold and pulled out a small handful of gold nuggets. I showed them to the Beard, but again all he did was look at my hand. His face showed no emotion. For a long time, I just sat with the Beard. We both moved only to stay in the shadow of the stones. I had forgotten how fierce the sun's rays are. Midou stayed at a distance, sorting through the carts and our equipment. He set up a trap for rodents with some scraps of dead ostrich, and then began to gather materials for a fire.

Eventually, the heat began to die down. The Beard opposite me was finally getting hungry. He reached down and snapped a small branch from a tree, which he began chewing. My patience was wearing thin. It was not the first time I had felt like an animal. I wanted to grab the branch from the Beard, shake him and demand he help us find food and water but I knew I had to wait and learn their ways. I glanced over at Midou. He had set up a tent and must have gone for a sleep.

The Beard did not seem to notice I was there. He finished his leafy snack and continued sitting with his eyes closed. The other Beards did the same. Sitting so still gradually helped me to forget my hunger and slaking thirst. But then the Beards began to stir. The sun was just setting. I looked up and saw the stars for the first time since Kerma. The Beards stood and stepped towards each other, looking up at the sky. Then they glanced over at Midou's fire. I could see they were curious. A couple of jerboas were feasting on the ostrich flesh. I left the Beards and caught one with the sole of my sandal whilst the other one scurried away. I skewered it with my knife and began to prepare it for roasting by burning off the hair and peeling off the top layer of skin. There is nothing worse than eating burnt hair. I cooked the jerboa and ate most of it, saving some for

Midou. I could hear his snoring and woke him with a short whistle.

The Beards were now moving sticks across the sand. It looked like they were plotting something. Midou chewed his jerboa. I lay down on the warm sand. The sky was dark but not quite yet black. It didn't take me long to realise these men were plotting the constellations. So they were holy men, priests of some sort? I watched Midou finish his last bite and wipe his mouth with the back of his hand. He was about to lie down again.

"What are you doing?" I asked. "We need water - more urgently than sleep!"

"I don't have the energy. But you're right. They must have a source somewhere."

Midou surprised me with his common sense. The nap must have done him good. He wandered back to our carts and grabbed two ostrich shells. Then he turned away began to pee in one of them. He brought it back to the fire, which was still burning well. He held the full eggshell over the flames and the other above it at a slight angle. The steam condensed into little drops of water and dropped down into the empty eggshell. There wasn't much, but it was enough to show the Beards what we needed. I winced slightly when one of the Beards drank from the eggshell. Midou kept pointing to it and I could hear him saying "Where?" over and over again in different tones of voice. The Beard turned his head and gave a look to one of the others. He walked off quickly and Midou followed after him.

I waited with the remaining Beards and saw their sand etchings. There were great holes linked by straight lines across the sand. I picked up Midou's eggshell and drank a few sips whilst trying not to draw attention to myself. It was enough to stop my face from feeling like it was swelling up.

Midou and the Beard stopped in the distance. They began circling around something – it must have been a well – and eventually they returned with two great buckets filled with water. The Beards shared one, handing it around. I felt like a dog. Finally, they gave the other one to me and Midou, who had already quenched his thirst. I drank as if my stomach were as big as the bucket.

I was hoping to sleep for a long time, but what happened next prevented me from sleeping at all that night. Midou returned to the tunnel entrance and brought both carts over. We only had one tent between us since we had lightened our load in Kerma.

Apart from the ostrich, there was nothing very useful left in our stores, just some spare clothes and basic tools.

The Beards lay on the sand to sleep. One of them had brought blankets from somewhere. I was curious to get a closer look at what they had been writing in the sand. Although the moon was out, it was just a crescent. I lit a torch from the dying fire and took it over to the standing stones. At first I could make out nothing in particular, just dots and lines in random directions. I looked up and saw a cluster of stars. They looked like a dog's face but with horns. A ram! I looked again at the sand and saw Khnum's face staring up at me.

We were a good distance from the river. Did the Beards know about the floods? They seemed quite happy with their well, although I didn't envy whoever had dug it out. It must have taken several years to pick at all that rock.

Something didn't add up. How did these men survive out here in the middle of the desert? Where were all the women and children? There must be a village close by. The Beards couldn't survive on water and plants alone. Yes they were thin, but not starving.

Just as my racing mind began to settle enough for sleep, I spotted what looked like a jackal, only slightly bigger. The Beards were on high alert. All seven of them stood up. Midou and I did the same but we weren't quick enough to act, having nothing to defend ourselves with. The creature came in for the kill. I darted towards the tunnel. The creature got caught in the obstacle course of the standing stones. I looked back and saw it clawing at something or someone. Midou and the other Beards had split. I climbed through the entrance to the tunnel. It was bitterly cold and I could hear the scratching of rodents.

In the dim moonlight, I could see something in the tunnel. Reaching out, I felt the rope we had used to pull our carts. Midou must have left it behind. I grabbed it and, in a bolt of courage, ran back across the sand to the site of the standing stones. One of the Beards lay screaming, kicking at the beast. I lashed out at it with the length of rope and it howled. The Beard screamed louder still as the giant jackal's claws sank into him. I whipped it again, this time across its neck. It felt brutal, horrible. The jackal went running, whimpering.

As my eyes adjusted, I saw the faces of the other Beards behind the standing stones. Midou stepped out of the darkness and sat down next to the wounded Beard. He grabbed the blanket lying next to him and began to wrap it around his legs. I couldn't see any blood but I knew it was there.

The other Beards joined hands in a circle and began to chant. The sounds were hard to make out but it was something like "*kim kin, kim kin*". They moved apart, still in a circle, and shook their hands high and then low.

"What are they doing?" I asked Midou.

"Praying?" Midou replied. He was helping the injured Beard to drink water from the bucket.

"We've got to keep moving," I said. "They hunt at night."

"You're right," said Midou. "We can sleep when it's hot."

Two Beards came over. They sat next to their bleeding friend and seemed to smile at us. Midou went off to the well and refilled our eggshells without any complaints. I packed up the tent and loaded the carts. As Midou was positioning the eggshells, one of the Beards came rushing over with two wooden buckets filled with water. We thanked the Beards and a few of them walked with us before waving us off into the night. I looked up and saw the constellation of Khnum above.

For days on end, we used the stars to guide us, always walking with the constellation of Khnum ahead of us. Walking at night helped. Our carts seemed to glide across the sand compared with when we were in the tunnels. My arms were becoming firm. They weren't anywhere near as thick as Midou's but I allowed myself some vanity to make up for the pain.

*

My heart sang when I first glimpsed Elephantine Island. It was dark and the islanders would still be in their beds. Would they even recognise me? My hair and beard were completely wild.

The island itself was humming with life – the banks were lush and green. The empire of Kerma, and the gruelling journey back from Nebu Island, was now a distant memory. Midou had gone to meet his new baby and see his wife for the first time in months. There was no one at the jetty so I headed home. My chamber was exactly as I had left it, except for a few dead scarab beetles. Then I saw something that made my throat tighten. My sundial had gone. The sundial Dad had made for me.

In the temple, there were more offerings than I had ever seen before. Flower heads, cups of wine and fresh bread were laid out next to brand new *stelae* depicting Khnum. The pharaoh's cartouche was etched next to it. In the corner of my eye, I saw sarcophaguses piled in the corner. There must have been at least twenty adult-sized coffins there. I shuddered as I said my prayers. The temple was empty and I was glad to get back outside into the warm air.

I went towards Wadi's shack. The place was deserted. A pile of shrivelled fruit told me that she had not been there for some time. Clothes were strewn on the floor and her comb lay on the bed, full of her long black hair. The room was musty and unpleasant. I noticed a new building nearby. It was a peculiar shape – rectangular – with a curved front entrance, a domed roof and large windows all around it. A wooden placard read:

NOME OF ELEPHANTINE ISLAND - under the governance of Zau.

I hopped over the wall and peered through the window. The place was empty except for a table and, on it, a large object covered in cloth. I climbed through the window, checking that no one was watching me. It was then that I heard a muffled birdcall coming from the table. My poor Seker! Removing the cloth from her cage, I saw she was tatty and thin. I snapped the wooden slats of her prison but she was too weak to fly. I had to get her some meat before she lost any more of her strength.

A narrow passage took me to the back room where various scrolls were piled high. As I rummaged through the paperwork – finding my letters amongst them – I spilled ink over the table. *For Khnum's sake.* I folded the scrolls flat and took them with me, Seker still cradled in my arms.

Outside, the islanders were up and busying themselves with their daily tasks. I held Seker closer and pushed on towards the beach. People I didn't even recognise called out my name. I could see they had been celebrating the return of the flood. Rams had been herded up and their horns covered in bracelets. I saw Nizam in the crowd. He was taller but his face was the same. Our eyes didn't meet. I walked on, half-lame from the journey. I spotted Nepthys looking tired and wan. She stared at me before looking away. To her, I was a stranger. I moved closer.

"Wait, Nepthys," I called.

She spun around.

"Harkhuf?"

Her eyes were older. She covered her mouth.

"Wadi's dead," she said. "I didn't even get to wrap her."

"Where's Zau?" I asked, my voice low and gravelly.

"He's gone. Nobody knows where."

My throat tightened as I pictured the face of the man I would need to destroy.

19

Harkhuf: A Hundred Friends

My journey to the City of the White Walls passed quickly. It was a perfect flood. The crops were still young and patchy but in a matter of weeks, there would be enough to go around again. For now, there was meat, wine and clean water at last. I wondered if, somewhere along the river's stretch, Dad was admiring it too. I travelled by taxi, stopping at night in guest houses, offering small pellets of gold as payment. I was welcomed by locals. My plan was to explain everything to the pharaoh in person: that Zau and my dad were missing, that I had written frequently and in good faith. Would he accept my story? What had Zau told him?

Nepthys's words still rang in my ears. *"Wadi's dead."* The drought had taken Wadi from me and there was only so much victory I could enjoy.

At the palace, I was met by a guard who led me straight to an antechamber filled with the sound of harp music. The harpist must have been Tepi – she was famous across the Black Land – and it was said that she could turn babies in the womb with her music.

Women travelled for miles in the hope of getting their little ones in the right position for birth. I recognised the rise and fall of the notes from songs Wadi had sung.

Tepi didn't look at me, she was so involved in her music. Her fingers sped over the strings with the lightest touch. I was mesmerised. Her harp was carved with angular lines like fish scales. The front had been made to look like Khnum: a ram head embellished with rubies for eyes. It was the first time I had seen carvings of Khnum anywhere but on Elephantine Island. I had a sense of being at home. Although I'd already been back to the island, I had not felt at home there. It's people that make a home, and my people were missing.

I heard a voice say my name and I turned to see the pharaoh himself in the doorway, looking at once bewildered and overjoyed.

"My wife told me you would return. Why do I never listen?"

I bowed and he took my hands in his and covered them in kisses.

"These are the hands of a pathfinder," he said.

I didn't have to explain a thing. Queen Ankhesen had sensed something was wrong and they had already sent a spy to monitor Zau before his disappearance.

"But we must waste no time in getting you back to Nubia to find your father before Zau does," the pharaoh said, rummaging through a pile of maps.

The thought of returning to Nubia made me feel about a hundred years old. I heard a baby wailing and soon learned that the royal prince had been born. He had been named Pepi II, after his grandfather. Queen Ankhesen was gleaming with happiness and wellbeing. I couldn't say the same for the pharaoh. The drought had dried up his spirit. He was spent. His priest, Seneni, had deserted him, and although Merenra was glad of the floods, he was still fretting about his tomb, which remained unfinished.

The drought may have lifted but it seemed the Black Land was still under threat, only this time it was from humans and not gods. If I can handle Khnum, I can take on Zau, I told myself. Dusting down my bag, I reached out and took the maps from the pharaoh.

Zau: Epilogue

Wadi slept for a long time. The journey had been long but the den made up for it. I'd built it with funds from Seneni. There was a panther skin rug, wooden furniture and an outdoor terrace sheltered from nosiness by bamboo panels.

Wadi was happy that she was helping me to help the pharaoh. She had recovered from her sickness but was still very thin. I knew her sister feared the worst but that was what I had planned. I didn't want her to come looking for us. I had to wrap up an old goat and lay it in the ground to stop Nepthys asking questions. I had instructed Nizam to stock the den with plenty of eggs, fish and bread. Breakfast was served on the terrace. I helped Wadi cut up her food. She was weak and tired, but the sleep had brought some colour back to her face. I think she was surprised to see Iry in the den but if anything, it was a comfort to her.

The sacrifice was ready. I had to get a message to Seneni urgently and I couldn't trust a messenger. We would have to go to the palace ourselves, and there was every danger of bumping into Harkhuf or, worse, reaching the City of the White Walls after he did. Our den was halfway between the island and the capital, and I had a reliable look-out in my new servant Nizam. The floods may have returned but it was only a matter of time before the pharaoh realised that a sacrifice was his only chance of making it to Duat.

Glossary of Old Kingdom Egyptian words and terms

Ankh	– the symbol of life
Black Land	– the fertile plains of the River Nile
Cartouche	– the pharaoh's seal as depicted in an inscription
Cubit	– an ancient unit of measurement, roughly equivalent to 30 cm
Duat	– the afterlife
Faience	– glazed ceramic
Festival of Wag	– an ancient festival celebrating the dead
Heka	– magic energy
Iteru	– The River Nile
Kalasiri	– woman's dress
Mana	– a person's individual power or energy
Medjay	– an ancient tribe living near the Red Sea
Nome	– an area of governance
Osiris	– Egyptian god of the afterlife, death, life and resurrection
Red Land	– the desert
Sakkara	– the ancient name for Saqqara
Senet	– an ancient Egyptian board game

Set	– Egyptian god of storms, desert, chaos and war
Setju	– an ancient Nubian settlement about halfway between modern-day Dongola and Wadi Halfa
Shamsi	– a Nubian bread
Shendyt	– skirt worn by men
Stelae	– wall engravings, often depicting a story of religious significance
Ta-Sety	– the ancient name for the region in the south bordering Nubia, which included modern-day Elephantine Island
White Walls	– the ancient name for Memphis

Acknowledgements

In no particular order, I would like to thank the following people for their assistance and support:

Lorna Stevenson, Professor Richard Parkinson, Philip Womack, Jonathan Buckley, James Marshall, Midou Turkey, Professor Alejandro Jiménez-Serrano (University of Jaén), Kate Brown, Mari D., Melvin Burgess, Joan Lennon, Lucy Norman, Beka Diski, Romain Brisson, Kim McNeil, Sophie Playle, Alexander Singleton, Eryl O'Day, Jill Steel, Andrew Steel, Simon Steel, Tim Freeman and Holly at *The Agency*.